David Pace qualified as an architec time as a children's author and illustrator. ew, lively illustrative style, moving away from 'tight' architectural forms. David illustrated *Emily and the Werewolf* for Liber Press and created a pop-up series for Oyster Books.

FOR MUM AND DAD, WITH LOVE

First published in Great Britain in 1995 by
Frances Lincoln Limited, 4 Torriano Mews
Torriano Avenue, London NW5 2RZ

British Library Cataloguing in Publication Data available on request

ISBN 0-7112-0895-6 – hardback
ISBN 0-7112-0896-4 – paperback

Printed and bound in Hong Kong

3 5 7 9 8 6 4 2

SHOUTING SHARON

A RIOTOUS COUNTING RHYME

DAVID PACE

FRANCES LINCOLN

One daring Desmond ready to dive,
and Sharon shouted . . .

JUMP!

Two tired twins asleep in a pram,
and Sharon shouted . . .

WAKE UP!

Three busy barbers snipping beards,
and Sharon shouted . . .

CUT!

Four fat ladies trying to slim,
and Sharon shouted . . .

CHOCOLATE!

Five French chefs cooking food for a feast,
and Sharon shouted . . .

YUK!

Six acrobats on a flying trapeze,
and Sharon shouted . . .

CATCH!

Seven proud dogs at a top-dog show,
and Sharon shouted . . .

CATS!

Eight explorers in a deep dark cave,
and Sharon shouted . . .

BEAR!

Nine brass bandsmen marching past,
and Sharon shouted . . .

HALT!

Ten lions licking their lips,

and Sharon shouted . . .

But nobody came . . .

The End

MORE PICTURE BOOKS IN PAPERBACK
FROM FRANCES LINCOLN

NUMBER PARADE
Jakki Wood

One slow tortoise, five rollicking rascally racoons, ten bouncing bopping wallabies . . . Jakki Wood's birds and beasts gain multiples and momentum as the score mounts to 101 in this wildlife counting book.

Suitable for National Curriculum, Mathematics - Level 1
Scottish Guidelines, Mathematics - Level A

ISBN 0-7112-0905-7   £4.99

ANIMAL PARADE
Jakki Wood

An exciting animal ABC featuring over 90 species parading nose-to-tail. With bright, charming watercolours, this unusual alphabet book will delight every young reader.

Suitable for National Curriculum English - Reading, Key Stage 1
Scottish Guidelines English Language - Reading, Level A

ISBN 0-7112-0777-1   £4.99

Frances Lincoln titles are available from all good book shops.
Prices are correct at time of publication, but may be subject to change.